For the wonderful people at Flying Eye Books,
who helped bring this book to life.

First edition published in 2021 by Flying Eye Books, an imprint
of Nobrow Ltd. 27 Westgate Street, London, E8 3RL.

1 3 5 7 9 10 8 6 4 2

Published in the US by Nobrow (US) Inc.
Printed in Poland on FSC® certified paper.

ISBN: 978-1-83874-064-1
www.flyingeyebooks.com

Ella Bailey

When I'm
BIG

Flying Eye Books

London | Los Angeles

Deep in a large, ancient forest, sat a small, lonely egg.

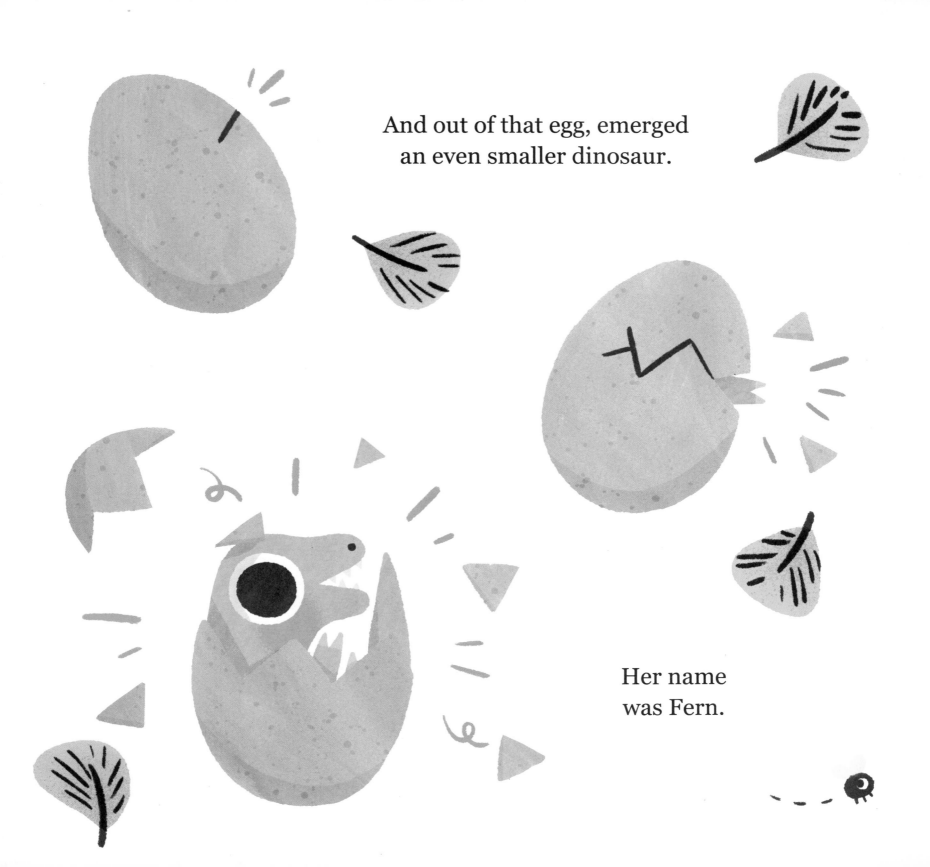

And out of that egg, emerged
an even smaller dinosaur.

Her name
was Fern.

Fern peered up at the towering
trees that surrounded her.

She saw that she was only as tall as the smallest fern frond.

"I'm small now," she thought, "but I wonder what I'll be like when I'm **BIG**."

Pondering this question, Fern spotted
an enormous dinosaur munching on
the treetops above her.

"Perhaps I'll grow taller than even
the **TALLEST** trees!" she wondered,
nibbling on a fallen leaf.

YUCK! Absolutely not!

"My neck is probably too short anyway," she reasoned, before going on her way.

But it was **MUCH** too noisy here for Fern's liking and she hurried off in search of some peace and quiet.

Fern then stumbled upon a wide, flowing river.
She noticed there were some strange, smooth
creatures dipping and diving within it.

"Oh, of course! When I'm **BIG**,
I'll live underwater!"

However, she soon learned that she wasn't really built for swimming...

...and grumbled as
she squelched away.

Everywhere she went, Fern kept her eyes peeled for a dinosaur that looked like something she might grow into.

"Will I sprout wings and soar high into the sky?"

"Will I have lots of pointy horns?"

"Will I be covered in awesome, bumpy armour?"

"Will I grow beautiful, bright feathers?"

But nothing felt right.

She was beginning to think she would never know
what sort of dinosaur she would become.

Heading back into the forest, Fern saw a group of dinosaurs not much bigger than her zipping across the path ahead.

"That's it. Maybe I won't grow **BIG** at all," she thought.

But before she'd even managed to introduce herself, they darted into the undergrowth without so much as a hello!

"How **RUDE**," said Fern. "Well ... I wouldn't want to be like you anyway!"

Exhausted, lonely and frustrated, Fern had given up hope.
Until she stumbled upon something that looked familiar.

"I know that egg!" she cried,
realising she was right back
where she started.

And Fern noticed something. Her old egg now looked so small, and the trees that once towered over her didn't seem so tall anymore.

"I've grown **BIGGER**!" she gasped with glee.

Fern knew now. She didn't need others to show her who she would be when she was big.

She could simply wait and see.

So that's what she did...

Deep in a large, ancient forest, sat a small egg.

Fern carefully covered
it with a fallen frond.

"You're small now," Fern
whispered to the little dinosaur
she knew was growing inside.

"But someday, you'll be BIG."

Did you spot all the dinosaurs?

Stegosaurus

Brachiosaurus

Ankylosaurus

Baryonyx

Parasaurolophus

Pachycephalosaurus